The Final Toast

by Stuart M. Kaminsky

SAMUEL
FRENCH

FOUNDED 1830

NEW YORK HOLLYWOOD LONDON TORONTO

SAMUELFRENCH.COM

Copyright © 2008 by Stuart M. Kaminsky

ALL RIGHTS RESERVED

CAUTION: Professionals and amateurs are hereby warned that *THE FINAL TOAST* is subject to a royalty. It is fully protected under the copyright laws of the United States of America, the British Commonwealth, including Canada, and all other countries of the Copyright Union. All rights, including professional, amateur, motion picture, recitation, lecturing, public reading, radio broadcasting, television and the rights of translation into foreign languages are strictly reserved. In its present form the play is dedicated to the reading public only.

The amateur live stage performance rights to *THE FINAL TOAST* are controlled exclusively by Samuel French, Inc., and royalty arrangements and licenses must be secured well in advance of presentation. PLEASE NOTE that amateur royalty fees are set upon application in accordance with your producing circumstances. When applying for a royalty quotation and license please give us the number of performances intended, dates of production, your seating capacity and admission fee. Royalties are payable one week before the opening performance of the play to Samuel French, Inc., at 45 W. 25th Street, New York, NY 10010.

Royalty of the required amount must be paid whether the play is presented for charity or gain and whether or not admission is charged.

Stock royalty quoted upon application to Samuel French, Inc.

For all other rights than those stipulated above, apply to Samuel French, Inc., at 45 W. 25th Street, New York, NY 10010.

Particular emphasis is laid on the question of amateur or professional readings, permission and terms for which must be secured in writing from Samuel French, Inc.

Copying from this book in whole or in part is strictly forbidden by law, and the right of performance is not transferable.

Whenever the play is produced the following notice must appear on all programs, printing and advertising for the play: "Produced by special arrangement with Samuel French, Inc."

Due authorship credit must be given on all programs, printing and advertising for the play.

ISBN 978-0-573-66377-2   Printed in U.S.A.   #8229

No one shall commit or authorize any act or omission by which the copyright of, or the right to copyright, this play may be impaired.

No one shall make any changes in this play for the purpose of production.

Publication of this play does not imply availability for performance. Both amateurs and professionals considering a production are strongly advised in their own interests to apply to Samuel French, Inc., for written permission before starting rehearsals, advertising, or booking a theatre.

No part of this book may be reproduced, stored in a retrieval system, or transmitted in any form, by any means, now known or yet to be invented, including mechanical, electronic, photocopying, recording, videotaping, or otherwise, without the prior written permission of the publisher.

IMPORTANT BILLING AND CREDIT REQUIREMENTS

All producers of *THE FINAL TOAST* *must* give credit to the Author of the Play in all programs distributed in connection with performances of the Play, and in all instances in which the title of the Play appears for the purposes of advertising, publicizing or otherwise exploiting the Play and/or a production. The name of the Author *must* appear on a separate line on which no other name appears, immediately following the title and *must* appear in size of type not less than fifty percent of the size of the title type.

RIVERPARK CENTER'S CANNON HALL

Executive Producer
ZEV BUFFMAN

Associate Producer
ROXI WITT

TEXAS GAS
TRANSMISSION, LLC

Presents

SherlockHolmes
The FINALTOAST
A world premier by Stuart M. Kaminsky

By Stuart M. Kaminsky
Directed by Mark Bellamy

THERE WILL BE A 15-MINUTE INTERMISSION

CAST

SHERLOCK	RAYMOND L. CHAPMAN*
MYCROFT	MICK WEBER*
MARCH	SEAN COOPER*
DR. WATSON	MARK MCCARTHY*
REGINA/ROSE DRAGLETON	AMY JEAN JOHNSON**
JONAH THRACE/NICHOLAS DRAGLETON	JEFF CUMMINGS*
CHARLIE CHAPLIN	BING PUTNEY*
TIM ELLY/TOOLE	SAM WOOTTEN**
JACK DAWES/APPLICANT #2	THAD MAYHUGH

Sound Design by Brian Burchett
Lighting Design by Paul Miller
Scenic Design by Brian Traynor
Costume Design by Susan Neason
Casting Director Jeanne Williams
Production Manager and Scenic Construction by Randy Buehler
Stage Manager Kathi Karol Koenig*
Assistant Stage Manager James Carringer*
Fight Choreographer Mark McCarthy
Properties by Mary Jane Bowles
Wardrobe Mistress Josephine Poe
Assistant Wardrobe Mistress Jessica Sprankle
SCENIC CONSTRUCTION CREW: Brenda Hauser, Bryan Cecil, Tammi Kidd, Wesley Buehler, Darrell Day,
Hugh Whittaker, Rhonda McEnroe, Aldena Hershberger, Larry Cook, Scott Galloway
STAGE CREW: Larry Cook, Cedric Watkins, John Hall, Mary Jane Bowles, Iryma Doyle, Amber Butler, Tammi Kidd,
David Loney, Hillary Chandler, Aaron Wheeler, Doug Sasse, Sara Jane Behl, C. Paul Kaufman

CREDITS

ssdc The Director is a member of the *Society of Stage Directors and Choreographers, Inc.,* an independent national labor union.

* Member of Actors' Equity Association, the Union of Professional Actors and Stage Managers.
** Equity Membership Candidate

CHARACTERS

SHERLOCK HOLMES, the great detective

JOHN WATSON, M.D., shares rooms with Holmes, chronicles his cases

MYCROFT HOLMES, older brother of Sherlock, spends most of his time at the exclusive Diagones Club

MALCOM MARCH, a young man determined to get the best of Holmes and then to kill him

CHARLIE CHAPLIN, street-wise, somewhere between 11 and 14. He is a Baker Street Irregular and a favorite of Sherlock Holmes

JONAH THRACE, wealthy man who lives in fear that someone is trying to kill him.

BROKEN NOSE TOOLE, murderous thug employed by Malcom March

REGINA, Jonah Thrace's housekeeper

TIMOTHY ELLY, exiled from Germany, he works for Jonah Thrace

ROSE, Malcom March's sister who is determined to help her brother kill Sherlock Holmes

NICHOLAS, husband of Rose

JACK DAWES, unfortunate employee of Jonah Thrace

FIRST ACTOR, his one-line performance doesn't fit

POLICEMAN, has nothing to say

Note: The same actor can play THRACE and NICHOLAS. In addition the same actor can play REGINA and ROSE. The same actor can play FIRST ACTOR, JACK DAWES and POLICEMAN.

ACT I

Scene One

(DR. JOHN WATSON sits at his desk in the parlor of the rooms he shares with SHERLOCK HOLMES at 221B Baker Street, London West. The light through the window slowly fades as Act I, Scene I is played out. Watson is writing, pausing from time to time to consider what he will say and taking a sip of tea and perhaps a bite from a small tray of biscuits.)

WATSON. *(reading)* "It was a summer day not three months past that Sherlock Holmes encountered what appeared to be an impossible crime committed by a brilliant conscienceless murderer. I was seated where I now sit when a very nervous young man was ushered in."

(A nervous young man who plays with his hat, turning it repeatedly enters through the hall door. WATSON stands.)

MARCH. Mr. Holmes?

WATSON. No, I'm Dr, Watson, Holmes's...

MARCH. *(nervously)* Oh, I know who you are. I'm Malcolm March. I'm familiar with your writings about Mr. Holmes. In fact that is how I found out about him. I only hope that he is as superior a consulting detective as you have presented though 'he smoked his pipe and drank his quart of beer' as the poet says.

*(**HOLMES**, who has been unseen until now, rises from the high-backed armchair which faces the fireplace. He is wearing a smoking jacket and smoking a pipe.)*

HOLMES. May your hope become reality, Mr....

(MARCH *shuffles across the room to shake* HOLMES' *hand.*

MARCH. March, Malcolm March. Mr. Holmes you must help me. The police have accused a good and innocent man. Jack couldn't have. I'm certain they will soon arrest him, but he couldn't have done it. No one could have.

HOLMES. And yet the deed was done. Calm yourself. Watson, perhaps our young visitor would like some tea and one of Mrs. Hudson's chocolate filled pastries.

MARCH. No, thank you.

(HOLMES *motions for* MARCH *to take a seat. He does.* HOLMES *leans against the mantle smoking.*)

HOLMES. I would like to hear what transpired in your own words.

MARCH. Yes, yes of course. Perhaps I should begin by telling you something of myself, I am... was in the service of Mr. Jonah Thrace.

HOLMES. I am aware of his unfortunate demise.

MARCH. Yes?

HOLMES. I also know that your employment with Jonah Thrace is recent, that you grew up on a small farm somewhere in the country around London, north of the city. You are left handed. I also know that you were in the army in India but not for long. You were released for medical reasons. You were employed by Mr. Thrace, who liked you from the start, and hired you as a secretary though you had little experience at such a profession. You applied for and took the job because you wanted and still want to escape your rural upbringing. Am I correct?

MARCH. *(astonished)* In every detail. I've told you none of this. You've been investigating me. Why?

(MARCH *puts his left hand in his pocket.*)

WATSON. No, he is simply enjoying playing with you. Tell him Holmes for God's sake.

MARCH. Tell me what?

HOLMES. You were once married when you were a teen-ager and still on the farm. The marriage was brief and ended over the eternal issue of money.

WATSON. Enjoy yourself Holmes, but please ease Mr. March's anxiety. March, you say you've read my little tales of my friend's exploits. You should be aware of his skills.

MARCH. Yes, of course. I'm sorry. But how did you know all that about...

HOLMES. Your left hand is calloused. Your right hand is not. The calluses do not extend to the ring and small finger. What causes such calluses? The handle of a sickle, the frequent use of a grooming brush? The look I gave your left hand also told me that you had worn a ring on the wedding finger. The ring is gone but it was too tight and it cut into the flesh of your finger leaving a faint permanent scar. The ring was cheap metal, the ring of a farm boy. You did not go to school yet you speak not like a farm boy but a professional. You joined the army to learn how to talk and act like an educated young man. You succeeded and earned a job with Jonah Thrace over other applicants by being charming.

WATSON. *(wearily)* India.

HOLMES. Oh yes, India. Your eyelids are slightly puffy and pink. You have been infected by Trachoma, a disease rarely seen in England but endemic in Africa and India. You've been treated with a mild borax solution commonly used in India but not Africa. Minute white traces of the treatment are evident in the corners of your eyes.

(WATSON moves to look at MARCH's eyes.)

WATSON. You are, of course, right Holmes. I should have noticed. I saw dozens of cases during my service.

HOLMES. Watson, as always dear fellow, you see but you do not observe.

MARCH. *(pleading)* Mr. Holmes. I saw you and Dr. Watson in Cornwall over a year ago. You had just solved the case which Dr. Watson called 'The Dancing Men.' You were brilliant. I need your great skills now.

HOLMES. Yes, I believe you do. Now please tell us what happened.

MARCH. Mr. Thrace was a bit of a recluse and quite fearful of being robbed or even attacked by people with whom he had business conflicts. He received a death threat the very evening before he was murdered.

*(Stage goes gradually dark as **MARCH** continues.)*

And, as the poet wrote, 'The morning wind began to moan, but still the night went on: through its giant loom the web of gloom crept till each thread was spun. And, as we prayed, we grew afraid of the justice of the sun'.

*(Then in one corner of the stage we see **JONAH THRACE** standing before a large door. **MARCH** is there with a saucer and cup in his hand.)*

THRACE. You are sure this room is secure?

*(**MARCH** is very patient, reassuring, calm.)*

MARCH. Yes Mr. Thrace.

THRACE A snake? A poisonous snake down the bell pull sash.

MARCH. You had that sealed

THRACE. Gas. Through the vent

MARCH. Sealed as well.

THRACE. Secret passage

MARCH. You know there is none.

THRACE. I could be hypnotized into suicide

MARCH. Can't be done. A hypnotized person cannot be made to commit an act he or she would not do as Mesmer has demonstrated.

*(**THRACE** is growing hand-wringingly distracted.)*

THRACE. They could pipe in deafening music that will cause my brain to explode

MARCH. Science does not yet permit this and Regina would certainly hear. You have given too much thought to this sir.

THRACE. *(almost a whisper)* A bomb?

MARCH. Tea.

THRACE. My gun is loaded?

MARCH. Yes sir, and on your beside table. Just have your tea, bolt the door and the windows and I'll have Regina spend the night directly outside your room.

*(***THRACE*** takes the cup and saucer, steps back into the bedroom, ***MARCH*** leaves and closes the door.)*

THRACE. Yes, yes, yes.

*(We hear a key turn and hear two heavy bolts slide into place. ***MARCH*** backs into the darkness. We hear ***MARCH****'s voice offstage.)*

MARCH. According to the maid, Regina, there was no sound all night from Mr. Thrace's bedroom, and she assures me that she is a very light sleeper. When Mr. Thrace did not answer her knocks when he was brought his breakfast, the cook was sent to get me while Regina stayed at the door.

*(***MARCH*** hurries to the door. ***REGINA*** steps back. ***MARCH*** bangs at the door.)*

MARCH. *(continued)* Mr. Thrace...Mr. Thrace...

(No answer. He tries to open the door but to no avail. Suddenly two men in work clothes rush in.)

MARCH. *(continued)* Jack...

*(The men hurl their shoulders at the door. Inside the bedroom, ***THRACE****'s head is turned to the side. The two men approach the bed which is now lighted. One of the men, ***JACK***, turns Thrace over...)*

JACK. Mr. Thrace. Mr.....

(THRACE lies over the covers with a knife in his neck. **MARCH** *and* **REGINA** *appear behind them.* **MARCH** *motions* **REGINA** *back so she won't have to see the bloody corpse.*

Lights down. Stage dark.)

MARCH. 'For the Lord of Death with icy breath had entered in to kill,' to quote the poet.

HOLMES. And then you examined the windows and doors?

MARCH. Yes, of course. All firmly locked from the inside. Tim Elly and Jack Dawes, the groom and stable man, who broke down the door will confirm it.

(Lights go up on the parlor revealing **HOLMES**, **WATSON** *and* **MARCH** *in their previous positions.* **HOLMES** *is now writing on a sheet of paper and eating a chocolate biscuit.)*

HOLMES. Thrace could have been given a strong sleeping draft. He could have been alive and sedated when the door was forced open. Dawes turned the body over. He might at that point have struck the fatal blow with a secreted weapon. Watson, would you be kind enough to take care of this for me?

*(**HOLMES** hands **WATSON** the sheet of paper.* **WATSON** *reads it and looks up puzzled.* **HOLMES** *meets his eyes and smiles.)*

WATSON. Certainly.

*(**WATSON** exits.)*

MARCH. Mr. Holmes, Dawes is a good man with a wife and full-grown children. He has neither the guile nor the motive for such an act.

HOLMES. But he might do it for someone else, someone who wanted revenge or would profit from Thrace's death.

MARCH. Regina and I will receive a very small sum from Mr. Thrace's will. The remainder of his estate goes to a cousin in Australia. Can you help me, Mr. Holmes?

HOLMES. I'm confident that I can. Do you have anything you wish to add Mr. March?

MARCH. Nothing I can think of. I assume you will want to talk to Jack and the household staff who were present.

(**HOLMES** *moves to the writing table where Watson had been sitting. He picks up a plate of biscuits and offers them to* **MARCH.**)

HOLMES. Mrs. Hudson is an outstanding baker and I have a tendency to overeat her temptations. Her chocolate confections are especially satisfying.

(**MARCH** *takes a biscuit.* **HOLMES** *puts the plate down and takes one too. Both men munch as the conversation continues.*)

HOLMES. I do not believe I'll be able to interview Jack Dawes. I believe he is dead. I believe the police already consider it a suicide. Fear of getting caught, remorse. It doesn't matter.

(**MARCH** *pauses in his munching.*)

MARCH. Jack dead? That's not possible. I left him no more than two hours past. How do you…?

HOLMES. I don't, but it is the only logical conclusion.

(**HOLMES** *holds out the plate so* **MARCH** *can take another biscuit. He does so absently. He is confused by Holmes' reasoning.*)

MARCH. No.

HOLMES. Yes.

(**WATSON** *returns.*)

WATSON. What have I missed?

HOLMES. Much of what I believe will be the first moments of our tale. I'll catch you up later. What have you found?

(**MARCH** *has risen to take another biscuit.* **WATSON** *hands the sheet of paper back to* **HOLMES.**)

WATSON. I telephoned the police at Grumbow. The livery

man, Jack Dawes is dead. Bullet to the brain. The police are confident that it is suicide. The gun was still in his hand when the police went to arrest him and discovered the body in the stable.

MARCH. Good Lord.

HOLMES. Mr. March, you may return to Grumbow and do what you can to comfort Jack Dawes' widow and settle Jonah Thrace's estate.

(**MARCH** *rises, shifts the biscuit to his left hand and shakes the hand of both* **WATSON** *and* **HOLMES**.)

MARCH. Thank you both. I'm sorry to have troubled you.

HOLMES. No trouble.

MARCH. It's been an honor and an education meeting you. I can't believe Jack Dawes killed Mr. Thrace.

HOLMES. Nor can I. Can you have Regina, Tim Elly and yourself here by eight tonight?

MARCH. 'We wait for the stroke of eight, each tongue thick with thirst. For the stroke of eight is the stroke of fate that makes a man accursed'

WATSON. Quoth the poet?

MARCH. Yes, and yes I can have them here.

HOLMES. Good.

(**MARCH** *exits. We hear his footsteps on the stairs.* **HOLMES** *goes to the window and parts the curtain slightly.*)

HOLMES. The second item in my note.

WATSON. Taken care of though it was hard to find one of your Baker Street Irregulars on such short notice.

HOLMES. Which one?

WATSON. The Chaplin boy.

HOLMES. Good. Charlie is a bright lad.

WATSON. What now?

(**HOLMES** *moves to take a biscuit, but there are no more.*)

HOLMES. We wait. You to ponder the conclusion of this case and its literary merit and I to savor the opportunity for performance when the moment arrives.

(**HOLMES** *goes back to his chair and sits.*)

HOLMES. Watson.

WATSON. Yes?

HOLMES. I have an important question for you.

(**WATSON** *is highly attentive.*)

WATSON. Yes?

HOLMES. Do you think Mrs. Hudson has any more of those chocolate pastries?

Scene Two

*(A card room in The Diogenes Club. This can be a simple blackout with three easy chairs. An older man, **MYCROFT HOLMES**, sits in one chair, hands folded on his lap, eyes closed. **WATSON** sit in one of the other chairs. **HOLMES** stands, perhaps paces. Mycroft's eyes remain closed. **HOLMES** in mid-sentence says…)*

HOLMES. …and so you see Mycroft I am facing an old and determined enemy.

MYCROFT. Organized society or polite decorum?

HOLMES. No, an individual.

MYCROFT. Process of elimination suggests…

(He pauses for a few seconds of thought.)

Moriarity, but that would be too obvious. I assume you refer to a character from one of your endeavors chronicled by the good Dr. Watson.

HOLMES. Correct as always.

MYCROFT. And what do you seek from me Brother Sherlock?

*(**MYCROFT** unfolds his hands, opens his eyes, and sits forward with a grunt to examine his visitors. He checks his pocket watch.)*

MYCROFT. It's nearly tea time. As you know, I do not miss tea time here at The Diogenes Club.

HOLMES. We'll not be much longer.

*(**HOLMES** sits.)*

MYCROFT. Long enough to sit.

HOLMES. You know what I want.

MYCROFT. You want me to confirm that the name you wish to give me is that of a person inextricably woven into your case.

HOLMES. Unless you would prefer to say the name.

MYCROFT. Milverton.

WATSON. Pardon me, but you can't be sure of that.

(**MYCROFT** *gives* **WATSON** *a tolerant and superior look. He may even sigh. He checks his pocket watch again.*)

MYCROFT. One has only to know your stories and to listen closely to Sherlock's description of the details of the situation and suspects.

(**MYCROFT** *holds up his left hand to* **SHERLOCK** *who nods in understanding.*)

HOLMES. He is certain and he is quite correct.

MYCROFT. I suspect you want more from me than the simple confirmation of the identity of Milverton. I'm confident you will reveal this to me in good time. Meanwhile, your murderer has gone to great lengths to achieve his ends. I suggest great caution.

HOLMES. We will exercise it.

MYCROFT. Good. I should hate to lose my only brother.

HOLMES. And I should hate to be lost.

MYCROFT. Would you like to join me at tea? I'm meeting with the Ambassador from Germany. We will have a delightful discussion of the new trade agreement. He will lie to me skillfully, but not skillfully enough. You'll enjoy it.

HOLMES. I must get back to my murder.

MYCROFT. Murder, the enterprise of criminals who lack the capacity for alternative solutions to their problems. I have always hoped that you might employ your considerable skills in the service of something more important than crime.

WATSON. And what might that be?

MYCROFT. Politics, foreign affairs, economics. The crimes in such dark corners of human endeavor are of much greater consequence than simple murder.

(**MYCROFT** *shakes his head and rises. So do* **HOLMES** *and* **WATSON**.*)

MYCROFT. My dear Dr. Watson, I am well aware of your affection for and loyalty to my brother. Please do your best to protect him in his continuing follies.

WATSON. I will.

MYCROFT. And, if you will in the future, and I hope you forgive me, chronicle his exploits with a bit more accuracy and a bit less adoration. Now the Ambassador awaits my company and I look forward to his entertainment.

*(**MYCROFT** touches **HOLMES**' shoulder as he exits.)*

WATSON. In our few encounters, I have been unable to determine whether your brother is being condescending or simply polite to me.

*(**HOLMES** is lost in thought, but manages to say…)*

HOLMES. Our case comes to a head Watson and I must consider the dangerous delicacy of the situation lest we unleash a ghastly conflagration.

Scene Three

*(Stage goes black. We hear the sound of a solo violin. Brahms perhaps. As the lights return, we see **HOLMES**, playing soulfully in his rooms. He is alone. The door opens slowly and a boy about 11 walks in. His clothes are a bit down-at-the-heels. He pauses entranced by the music, then sneaks to the desk to filch a sandwich.)*

HOLMES. *(Without looking to the boy...)* Charlie.

*(***HOLMES*** finishes, points to the table. The boy advances and takes a trio of small sandwiches from a plate. **CHARLIE** nods his thanks, neatly folds the napkin around the sandwiches and places them in his pocket. **HOLMES** puts the violin and bow away carefully in an open case and sits. **CHARLIE** taps his pockets.)*

HOLMES. Your mother is back home.

*(His fingers are steepled. ***CHARLIE*** looks at the plate of sandwiches. ***HOLMES*** nods for him to take more. The boy does. ***CHARLIE*** sits deeply in Watson's chair.)*

CHARLIE. How'd you know about me mum being back home?

HOLMES. You've folded the napkin neatly. You're hoping for a response when she sees your gift. Were the sandwiches only for you, you would not have worried about protecting them from lint.

CHARLIE. It's creepy how you do that.

*(***HOLMES*** takes a cane from next to the fireplace and, a la The Little Tramp, twirls it as he loses himself in thought.)*

HOLMES. Is it? I suppose it is. Are you still planning to take to the stage like your mother?

CHARLIE. Could be.

*(***CHARLIE*** leaps from the chair and does a few dance steps ending with a perfect cartwheel.)*

HOLMES. Don't. No one can make a reasonable living from the stage. So, what did you find?

(HOLMES carelessly leans the cane against the wall. CHARLIE is back in the chair eating sandwiches.)

CHARLIE. Broken Nose Toole, nasty sort of big bloke and the other one. They talked. I got close enough to hear a bit.

(He clears his throat and changes his voice.)

'Why don't I just drop him?' 'No, I want him alive till... I want him to know. I want him to know he's lost.' 'Suit yourself.' That's about it Mr. Holmes.

HOLMES. I may have to revise my opinion of your making a living on the stage. You have a talent for mimicry.

(CHAPLIN shrugs, makes a little bow and keeps eating. The door opens and WATSON enters.)

WATSON. Holmes?

HOLMES. Please.

WATSON. This way please

(WATSON casts a disapproving eye at CHAPLIN in his chair. CHAPLIN rises, offers WATSON a sandwich. WATSON refuses with a shake of his head. The door swings open further. MARCH, REGINA and TIM ELLY enter. ELLY looks particularly uneasy. WATSON cuffs CHARLIE's head as the boy gets back in Watson's chair. CHARLIE vacates the chair so REGINA can sit. CHARLIE moves to the wall.)

HOLMES. Please find yourselves seats. You are Mr. Elly and you are Regina.

REGINA. I...

HOLMES. It was not a question. It was an observation.

(CHARLIE picks up the cane and twirls it as Holmes had done. He is delighted by the prop and continues to play with it.)

REGINA. What is this all about?

HOLMES. I'm trying to save a life, perhaps many lives. We are dealing with a brilliant, ruthlessly violent and very unbalanced murderer.

REGINA. Jack Dawes is dead. He was the murderer and I can tell you he was not a genius.

(**HOLMES** *lights a pipe.*)

HOLMES. Watson.

(**WATSON** *picks up a pad of paper from his desk and reads.*)

WATSON. Jane Phillipson, now known as Regina, has been dismissed from private employment four times, each under suspicion of theft. She has forged her references and somewhat changed her appearance.

(**REGINA** *shrugs, sits and folds her arms.*)

REGINA. That doesn't make me a murderer.

HOLMES. No, it does not. That brings us to Tim Elly.

(**ELLY** *looks at* **REGINA** *and* **MARCH.**)

MARCH. 'Quiet we sat and dumb, but each man's heart beat thick and quick like a madman on a drum.'

HOLMES. Your poet again.

MARCH. Yes, I'm sorry.

(**WATSON** *reads further.*)

WATSON. William Timothy Elly, a German citizen who was exiled from his native land for unspecified deviant behavior. He is married and has two small children.

(**WATSON** *looks up to be sure his words have registered.*)

Malcolm March, no other names. You most ably reduced his life to a few words when he was here this morning.

HOLMES. Oh yes, farm boy, India, Borax...

(**HOLMES** *waves away the words.*)

My puzzlement about this pair of murders was a result of being unable to find a motive. Then I realized I was looking in the wrong place. Mr. Chaplin supplied me with the missing piece of information, the motive, one that will haunt me long after I've retired to my apiary.

*(**CHARLIE** continues to hold the cane.)*

CHAPLIN. Raising bees.

HOLMES. I knew who the killer was moments after you first entered this room Mr. March. Your very first words provided the clue.

MARCH. My first words? What were they and who is the killer?

HOLMES. You are the killer and your very first words were, "Mr. Holmes?" Watson has already admirably recorded the process by which I came to this conclusion. Should you like to hear it?

CHAPLIN. Bloody well yes.

*(**WATSON** clears his throat and reads.)*

WATSON. "When March entered the room taking small careful steps, he seemed to mistake you for me," said Holmes. "Yet we look nothing alike and a few minutes later, March said that he had seen us at Cornwall. Why then would he pretend that he did not know what I looked like?"

MARCH. I…

*(**HOLMES** closes his eyes and holds up his hand for silence.)*

WATSON. "I then decided to check my observation," said Holmes. "I did this by making a series of deductions about March which I expressed. Some of them were correct, the presence of Trachoma, and some completely without foundation, March's having grown up on a farm for example. The number of ways a person could have acquired one particularly calloused hand are numerous."

CHAPLIN. Curtain pulley men favor one hand and it wears more than the other.

HOLMES. See. There's one. But you did not point out that I was wrong. You wanted me to think I was right. And I said you had a permanent scar from a cheap wedding band. There is no scar, just a small recent scratch above the ring line.

CHAPLIN. Could you learn me how to do that figuring out stuff?

HOLMES. 'Teach' you, not 'learn you'.

CHAPLIN. Teach me then.

HOLMES. I do not think I would find that professorial duty rewarding. Now, if you will pardon me, I am in the process of trapping a murderer.

*(**REGINA** remembers.)*

REGINA. The locked room?

HOLMES. The locked room.

*(The lights go on and again we see the bedroom of **JONAH THRACE** where the enactment of Holmes' version of the murder as he gives it takes place.)*

March here poisoned Jonah Thrace, who had enough time to lock the door and get to bed, where he died. Arsenic likely diluted with a sleeping draught would do quite well. When the door was broken down the next morning, it was not Jack Dawes who was first to enter but Malcolm March who approached the body, took a knife from his pocket or, more likely, where he had hidden it in the bed the night before. He stabbed the already dead Thrace and stepped back to allow Dawes to turn the dead man over. The story of Jack Dawes murdering Jonah Thrace was a lie.

(Lights are back up. We are in Holmes' and Watson's parlor again.)

WATSON. The police would never look for evidence of poison since Jonah Thrace was obviously stabbed.

REGINA. What about Mr. Elly here? He saw Jack turn Mr. Thrace over.

HOLMES. I believe Mr. Elly and his family have been threatened by the innocent looking Mr. March. Elly knows what March is capable of. Mr. Elly is living in fear.

CHAPLIN. Right enough. But March here'll cut his throat soon enough given a bye-your-leave.

(**ELLY** *sits, hands shaking, unable to meet the eyes of* **MALCOLM MARCH**.)

REGINA. But why would he do it? He gets almost no money?

HOLMES. Young Mr. Chaplin here followed March who met with another man. The man told of wanting to kill someone at March's behest.

ELLY. Me. He plans to kill me?

HOLMES. No, Mr. Elly. He plans at some point in the near future to kill me.

(**MARCH** *has now risen and moves to the plate of sandwiches. He takes one and eats without a care.*)

MARCH. And why would I want to do that?

HOLMES. To demonstrate to yourself and to me that you are more clever than I. However, that can't be done without my knowing what you've done. Your motive is simple. Revenge. And you wanted to "get the best of" Sherlock Holmes before you killed him.

CHAPLIN. You bollixed it mate.

MARCH. Why would I want to murder someone just to best you Holmes? I'd have to be mad.

HOLMES. And that is precisely what you are. And your father was. If I am not mistaken, you are the son of Charles Augustus Milverton.

MARCH. And what makes you think this?

HOLMES. Your eyes are the same intense grey and your last two fingers on your left hand are, like your father's, the same length. You did your best to keep your hand casually in your pocket which was all the more reason for me to examine it when you did show it.

MARCH. You think I waited two years to get revenge?

HOLMES. Not by choice. You were in prison where you did not behave. Those short steps you take indicate prolonged attachment of leg irons. Your pale skin suggests solitary confinement. You had plenty of time to read or listen to your poet and go mad. All the poetic passages you have quoted are from Mr. Oscar Wilde's recently published 'Ballad of Reading Gaol'. I think I may safely conclude that you were in Reading Gaol in some proximity to Wilde as he wrote.

CHAPLIN. *(to* **MARCH***)* Went a bit clocky wearing the Broad Arrow you did.

HOLMES. 'The vilest deeds like poison weeds bloom well in prison air', according to your Mr. Wilde.

(Long pause while **MARCH** *decides how to handle this.)*

MARCH. I watched Wilde slowly fall into deep despair and felt pity, but you both stood by and watched my father being murdered and did nothing to save him.

WATSON. He was shot by a poor woman he had blackmailed and whose life had been brought to ruin. There was nothing we could do to intervene.

MARCH. So you wrote, but I've read your account and your most unflattering description of my father. The great Sherlock Holmes could have saved him.

HOLMES. He was a diabolical and worthy opponent. You suffer from a rage that keeps you from joining the ranks of villains such as Moriarty, Colonel Moran, or even your father.

MARCH. *(amiably)* You called my father The Worst Man in London. I am his son and heir and avatar.

WATSON. You are also a murderer who is about to be turned over to the police.

MARCH. Perhaps another time.

(He takes out a gun.)

I've never killed a child before, but I think I'll take particular delight in getting rid of this one. You, Holmes, I will not kill now. I intend to leave you here midst four corpses. You will have failed to save the lives of six people. I would like to think that you would take your own life, but you are a remorseless bastard.

(He takes aim at Watson. **CHAPLIN** *tumbles in front of* **MARCH**, *knocks him over and whacks the gun from* **MARCH**'s *hand with the cane.* **REGINA** *and* **ELLY** *sit frozen as* **WATSON** *picks up the dropped gun and aims it at* **MARCH**'s *face.)*

WATSON. That was closer than I like.

MARCH. You think this is the end? You self-centered, pompous, smug, priggish…

*(***MARCH*** searches for more insults. Holmes looks at the clock on the mantle.)*

WATSON. Conceited?

CHAPLIN. Hoity-toity?

HOLMES. I'm sure March is grateful for assistance, but the police are downstairs?

CHAPLIN. Just like you asked, Mr. Holmes.

MARCH. I will outlive you Sherlock Holmes. That will bring justice and justification for my father and for me. You think me mad? You have yet to see what determination true madness can bring.

*(***WATSON*** escorts ***MARCH*** out the door. ***MARCH*** is grinning quite madly.)*

REGINA. Believe me Mr. Holmes, I knew nothing about any of this.

HOLMES. You are believed. The police will want to talk to you both on the way out.

ELLY. I was a coward Mr. Holmes, but I've got the wife and children. All I did in Germany was buy and try to read a book by a poet, Heinrich Heine. The police in my town said it was a perversion. I didn't even understand the book.

HOLMES. I care nothing of this but as for saving the life of Jack Dawes, you could have taken care of the problem without telling me or the police.

ELLY. What?

HOLMES. You could have killed Malcolm March.

ELLY. Murder?

HOLMES. Execution. Good day Mr. Elly.

REGINA. I have no excuses or threats to make and I require no lessons from you. I was fortunate in finding employment with Mr. Thrace and I will find a new position in another household.

HOLMES. I wish you well. Oh, by the way, I strongly suggest that you return the jewelry you have taken from Mr. Thrace's drawers before the police search your person.

(REGINA fixes a cold eye on Holmes but can't hold the look. She shakes her head, removes jewelry from her pockets and places it on the desk.)

It made a most conspicuous bulge and your hands in your pockets played almost lasciviously with them. Whatever is in your handbag too. Had you room in the handbag, this jewelry would have been there.

(REGINA empties more items from her pocketbook and places them on the desk.)

REGINA. The gold in my teeth is my own.

HOLMES. And it gives you a fetching smile.

(ELLY and REGINA exit leaving HOLMES and CHAPLIN who stands at the door.)

CHAPLIN. This was better than music hall.

(HOLMES takes a coin out of his pocket and flips it to CHAPLIN who pockets it and tosses the cane to HOLMES who tosses it back to the boy.)

HOLMES. It's yours.

(CHARLIE does a dance step with the cane, pivots and exits splay-footed like The Little Tramp. HOLMES picks up a sandwich, tastes it and smiles. There is a shot offstage. HOLMES moves to the window and looks out. WATSON bursts through the door gun in hand. He is panting.)

WATSON. He got away.

(**HOLMES** *is still looking out.*)

HOLMES. So I see. He is quite swift.

WATSON. The police are in close pursuit. They'll soon have him.

HOLMES. I think not, Watson. This is not the end of our tale. When young Malcolm March is dead, you will have your ending. I believe I'll have one more bite and...

(**HOLMES** *picks up the violin and starts to tune it. Stage goes dark. We hear the sound of a violin soulfully playing, perhaps something by Brahms. as the lights rise on...*)

Scene Four

(The Card Room at The Diogenes Club. **MYCROFT** *has a book open in front of him. A pair of spectacles is perched on the end of his nose. He takes of sip from a glass of wine on the small table next to him. The door opens. A dignified old man in an impeccable suit enters quietly and walks slowly across the room toward to the book shelves. It is* **MALCOLM MARCH** *in disguise, and a fine disguise it is too.)*

MARCH. Sorry.

*(***MYCROFT*** grumbles acknowledgement and goes on reading.* **MARCH**, *now with book in hand, moves to the seat across from* **MYCROFT**.*)*

You mind?

MYCROFT. No.

MARCH. You a card player?

MYCROFT. No.

MARCH. This is the card room.

MYCROFT. And one of the few rooms in the Club where one can be alone.

MARCH. I'm sorry. I find cards to be a passing diversion. I expect the various games will fade as quickly as they have come.

*(***MYCROFT*** looks up.)*

MYCROFT. A century ago a Mr. Barrington found evidence that Edward I played cards as early as 1278. The confirmed history of cards began in 1393 when three packs of cards, jeux de cartes were purchased in Paris for the amusement of King Charles VI, who had lost his mind the previous year. In 1463, parliament issued a ban on the importation of cards to protect domestic manufacturers. Henry VIII lost thousands from the privy purse at cards and Mary was a constant card player during her entire reign though she supported a statute in 1541 forbidding the playing of cards by the lower classes. Games of cards have been mentioned in literature since Gammer Gurton's Needle.

MARCH. I'm sorry I didn't appreciate the importance of the game in our history.

MYCROFT. You are not.

MARCH. Not?

MYCROFT. You are not sorry. You are certainly not interested.

(**MARCH** *gets up and moves to the door as if to leave because of the insult, but instead he locks the door and turns to face* **MYCROFT** *who has gone back to his reading.*)

Two more lines.

(*He reads, puts a bookmark in his book, places the book on his lap and removes his spectacles.*)

The German government has always been highly predictable.

(**MARCH** *moves back toward* **MYCROFT**.)

MARCH. Interesting.

MYCROFT. You, however, are not predictable.

MARCH. And why is that?

MYCROFT. Because you are quite mad, March.

(**MARCH** *removes most of his disguise and sits across from* **MYCROFT** *again.*)

MARCH. Would you like to pontificate about the history of madness?

MYCROFT. It is of no interest to me. My brother, I am sure, possesses a far more extensive knowledge of the subject.

MARCH. You know why I am here?

MYCROFT. Yes.

MARCH. You think I'm going to kill you.

MYCROFT. No. I think you have already sent word to Sherlock that you have me here at the point of a...

(MARCH removes a gun from his pocket and aims it at MYCROFT.)

…a Derringer pocket pistol I believe.

(There is a knock at the door. MARCH rises, gun aimed at MYCROFT, and moves toward the door.)

MARCH. Who is it?

HOLMES. The Bastard King of England here to claim the throne. March, you know full well who it is.

(MARCH opens the door and turns his gun on HOLMES who enters and closes the door behind him.)

HOLMES. *(continued)* Mycroft, are you all right?

MYCROFT. Perfectly. I was just admiring March's weapon.

HOLMES. A poor but effective copy of those made by Henry Derringer. The one in March's hand is a Slotter pistol.

MYCROFT. I think you wrong on this one Sherlock. The gun in March's hand is a Derringer like the one Booth used to kill the American President.

(HOLMES moves past MARCH to engage his brother in closer discussion.)

MARCH. Stop it. It doesn't matter who made the gun. It is effective in its missions.

HOLMES. It fires only one shot.

MARCH. And I have two guns.

(He removes a second gun from his pocket, also a Derringer.)

I obtained them as a pair and I can assure you they are effective. I've had reason to use them.

(HOLMES moves to the side of MYCROFT who remains seated.)

Please move to the window. Both of you.

(HOLMES and MYCROFT comply.)

What do you see?

HOLMES. A tall man and a boy on the street corner.

MARCH. And do you recognize the boy?

HOLMES. Chaplin.

MARCH. Should I not depart this building alone, should I wave from the window, the boy's throat will be cut. As Mr. Wilde wrote…

MYCROFT. Please do not quote from that unfortunate deviant writer of epigrams and doggerel. Shoot me if you must, but spare me the poetry.

(**MYCROFT** *and* **SHERLOCK** *continue to look out the window.*)

HOLMES. The man across the street professes to be Catholic, but he is not.

MYCROFT. He suffers an extreme alcohol addiction.

HOLMES. And its effect on his liver are in the final stages.

MARCH. Stop it.

(**MYCROFT** *and* **HOLMES** *ignore March's plea.*)

MYCROFT. He has some difficulty keeping his head erect.

HOLMES. There is a yellowish caste to his skin which can be seen even at this distance.

MARCH. Stop it.

MYCROFT. He has a tremor in both hands, slight but detectable.

HOLMES. His right hand is almost imperceptibly rubbing his stomach directly over his liver.

HOLMES. & MYCROFT. He is in pain.

MARCH. Stop it! Stop it both of you. That has nothing to do with my being here. Let it suffice that he…Would either of you like to guess what I plan to have happen here?

HOLMES. No guess is necessary.

MYCROFT. None. Two single shot pistols. A child hostage. You want us to shoot each other.

MARCH. Correct. But not before I have my say.

MYCROFT. And what makes you think I value the life of a street urchin more than my own? I still have work of some moment to do for my country. The boy will live his life on the back streets of London and will probably become a criminal. I'd be doing society a favor to shoot you and lament the passing of the boy.

MARCH. Your brother doesn't feel the same, do you Holmes?

HOLMES. No. I believe my brother underestimates the boy.

(**MARCH** *now has a gun in each hand. He moves around the room as he speaks. He goes to the window, looks out, keeps moving.*)

MARCH. My father was a brilliant man, a man who had…

MYCROFT. Shoot us. It is preferable to listening to you ramble on. Sherlock, I'll not forgive you for bringing your sordid business to me and in The Diogenes Club.

HOLMES. Sorry, but at the moment it would be best to address our situation.

MARCH. I have something to say to you bastards.

(**MYCROFT** *rises from his chair.*)

MYCROFT. Such language is not permitted within these walls.

(**MARCH** *laughs.*)

MARCH. What are you going to do, expel me? Deny my application for membership?

MYCROFT. Members do not apply. They are invited.

MARCH. Here are the pistols.

(*He hands them to* **MYCROFT** *and* **HOLMES**.)

If you have something more to say, say it but for the devil's sake, make it brief.

HOLMES. There are three ways out of this situation.

MYCROFT. Four. First, we shoot each other, but not fatally.

MARCH. I will regard that as a violation of my order and wave at the window.

HOLMES. We could restrain you if it weren't for the third and more serious weapon in your arsenal.

(**MARCH** *removes a pistol from his belt.*)

Of course, we could both shoot you.

MARCH. And when I failed to walk out the door downstairs the boy would die.

MYCROFT. I assume Dr. Watson stands ready outside the door. And the police.

HOLMES. Yes, Chief Inspector Lestrade himself, but if they were to enter, the problem of March's exiting the Club would still stand.

MARCH. I expect to be caught, but I will go to the gallows vindicated if I know you are dead Holmes.

MYCROFT. I assume we agree on our fourth alternative.

HOLMES. We do.

(**MYCROFT** *nods agreement.*)

You will walk out of here and wave off your cutthroat.

MARCH. I will not. Now, if you don't fire at each other, point blank, in the face by the count of three, no make that the count of ten. I want to savor your anguish. By the count of ten or the boy dies and so do both of you. One…

HOLMES. You walked into the Club in your admirable disguise. That is the way your accomplice last saw you.

MARCH. Two…

MYCROFT. And so you have inadvertently provided Sherlock with the opportunity to enter into another of his music hall performances.

MARCH. Three…

HOLMES. We will shoot you in both legs so that you cannot get to the window. Your accomplice will hear the two shots, believe the deed is done and wait for your appearance.

MARCH. Four…

MYCROFT. I find this solution distasteful, but it has minimal risk and the circumstances are singular. We do have an excellent physician in residence, Sir Desmond Phipps.

(It begins to dawn on **MARCH** *that they are seriously planning to shoot him.)*

MARCH. Five…?

HOLMES. Phipps, oh yes. Saved the life of the American ambassador. He must be nearing ninety.

MYCROFT. But his hand is still quite steady.

HOLMES. Dr. Watson might have a more steady hand.

*(***MARCH** *has had enough.)*

MARCH. I'll not be deprived of my satisfaction.

(He levels his pistol at **HOLMES** *and is about to fire.* **MYCROFT** *fires first.* **MARCH** *crumples to the floor.* **HOLMES** *fires the gun in his hands into the floor and steps forward to take the gun from the fallen* **MARCH** *who is holding his leg.)*

MYCROFT. If you had put the bullet into him, there would be no hole in the floor that I will have to explain to the board of directors.

HOLMES. Sorry.

*(***WATSON** *enters.)*

WATSON. Holmes are you…?

HOLMES. Quick Watson his coat. You really must stop flourishing guns March. The result seems to inevitably be that you wind up on the floor disarmed.

MYCROFT. I hope there isn't too much blood on the carpet, it was a gift from the Prince of…

*(***WATSON** *starts to remove March's coat and puts it on* **HOLMES***. They need not remove his dark pants.)*

WATSON. What is going on?

HOLMES. I'll explain later. We haven't a moment to lose. Lestrade?

WATSON. In the downstairs hall. I fear our presence here is not welcome.

MYCROFT. It most assuredly is not.

MARCH. Next time, Holmes. And there will be a next time…

(**HOLMES** *removes the false beard and glasses from March's pocket.*)

HOLMES. I should not be giving advice to the enemy, but if you want to succeed, keep it simple. You have an unfortunate predilection for the convoluted.

(**MYCROFT** *has cautiously gone to the window and pulled back the curtain just enough to see.*)

MYCROFT. Our alcoholic accomplish is looking up. You had best hurry.

(**HOLMES** *does.*)

When he entered, he had a slight flaw in his gait, his left leg.

HOLMES. I'll demonstrate it for you.

(*He does.*)

MYCROFT. Precisely. The prison shackles.

MARCH. I'll come back from the grave if I must.

HOLMES. And I'll be most interested if you do. Mycroft, can we do anything for you?

(**MYCROFT** *is back in his chair, book on his lap, glasses on his nose.*)

MYCROFT. Take all these weapons, depart and do not return.

(**HOLMES** *is donning the disguise.*)

HOLMES. How do I look so far?

MYCROFT. Like Sherlock Holmes in another of his childish disguises.

WATSON. Will someone please tell me what is going on?

HOLMES. The end of an act in our drama of Malcolm March.

MARCH. I'll come back for you, Holmes. I'll come back.

(*His voice rises.*)

I'll come back.

(**MYCROFT** *addresses* **MARCH.**)

MYCROFT. You are singular in your obsession and rather annoyingly repetitive.

MARCH. I'll recrudesce for you Sherlock Holmes. Is that better?

MYCROFT. Not as dramatic, but at least a variation.

(**HOLMES** *pauses to lift a glass of wine to* **MYCROFT** *in a toast.*)

HOLMES. With thanks for your assistance.

(**HOLMES** *drinks. Stage goes dark.* **MARCH** *'s voice fades to a threatening whisper.*)

MARCH. I'll come back.

Curtain

ACT II

Scene One

(WATSON sits at his desk revising with pen in hand. The only light comes from the dying embers in the fireplace. He reads…)

WATSON. "Several weeks passed without incident. I was nearly dozing…

(WATSON makes a correction)

I was unusually alert in spite of the lateness of the hour when… "

(HOLMES enters and removes his cape. WATSON puts down the pages and pen. HOLMES sits across from him in a straight-backed chair. WATSON, now alert, looks searchingly at HOLMES. Something is decidedly off in Holmes' appearance.)

WATSON. *(continued)* Holmes. I thought you'd almost be in Glasgow by now. Why are you back? You look…

HOLMES. What is it John? You look as if you've seen…

WATSON. Nothing Holmes. Nightmare. Surprise at seeing you, that's all.

(HOLMES rises suddenly.)

HOLMES. A good cigar, John. Shall we smoke in the darkness while I tell you of the singular adventure that began this day?

(HOLMES moves to the humidor on the mantle next to unanswered correspondence secured in the dark wood by a jackknife. HOLMES opens the humidor and shakes the empty can. He says wearily…)

HOLMES. It seems we will have to forgo the pleasure of tobacco.

WATSON. *(yawning)* Pity, but you have never been particularly dependent upon the weed in any case. I'd offer you a cigarette, but you never…

(**HOLMES** *waves the offer off, returns to the chair and crosses his legs as* **WATSON** *rises rather languidly.*)

HOLMES. Quite true. I'd like to get to the heart of my misadventure. As you know, I received a letter imploring me to come to Glasgow immediately and in the letter…

WATSON. …was a ticket for the train and a sum in cash.

(**WATSON** *moves to a drawer near the window. His back to* **HOLMES**.)

HOLMES. Seventy pounds. John, please stop fussing and sit down.

(**WATSON**, *hands in the pockets of his Randipur smoking jacket sits again, attention focused on* **HOLMES**.)

WATSON. Sorry, Sherlock. Just looking for something for you to eat. There are half a dozen boiled eggs in the sideboard but I know how you feel about…

HOLMES. I can do without the residue of barnyard fowl. Shall I tell you of this case or not. I must say, John, you seem oddly preoccupied whereas I anticipated that you would be agog over a new conundrum about which you might write.

WATSON. You have no idea how intrigued I am by your whereabouts this day. But may I first ask you what I believe to be a most important question?

HOLMES. Ask away, my dear fellow.

(**WATSON** *removes his Revolver from his pocket and aims it at Holmes' chest.*)

WATSON. Who are you?

HOLMES. Who am… Good Lord, John, how much have you had to drink. I'm Sherlock.

WATSON. Sherlock Holmes never calls me John. And he never permits anyone but his brother Mycroft to call him Sherlock. In addition, Sherlock Holmes knows full well that the cigars are kept not in the humidor but in the coal-scuttle. Sherlock Holmes has a passion for eggs. Sherlock Holmes would not refuse a cigarette when he was involved in a case. In fact, he would accept any form of tobacco.

HOLMES. Pray continue.

WATSON. The light is poor, but I can see that your nose is a bit too sharp, your hair a bit too dark, your cheeks a jot too full and there's something about...

HOLMES. ...the way I walk and talk?

WATSON. Exactly. You are a devilish approximation I admit, but I know Holmes too well. Now tell me what has become of the real Holmes or I shall fire with no hesitation.

*(**HOLMES** laughs deeply.)*

HOLMES. You missed several things Watson. For example, my walk. Most people walk listing very slightly to one side or the other depending on which hand they favor. In the elderly, it is far more pronounced. I list neither way. Placed in a desert, any human will walk in a circle. The left-handed will walk to the right. Actually, the diameter of the circle of a wandering man should tell you his approximate age and height. General Kitchener...

WATSON. Rubbish. Where is Holmes?

*(**HOLMES** removes a pipe from his pocket and picks up the Persian slipper on the table. He fills the pipe with tobacco.)*

HOLMES. I also put lifts in both of my shoes to give me an extra inch over my normal height. The weapon you are holding is a 2 1/2-inch barrel, 442 model 1872. It requires no ejector rod. Spent cases are extracted by removing the cylinder entirely, a rather cumbersome method which makes the weapon a chore to fire and clean. You don't wish the boredom of cleaning such a weapon and, as I know, the last time you fired it was two years ago to kill the unfortunate giant rat of the Sumatra. You are possibly not even sure if a spent round now resides in each chamber. Are you satisfied Watson?

WATSON. Not in the least. But I am impatient.

(The door to the landing opens. A figure stands in the shadows. **WATSON** *turns his gun toward the figure who emerges into the light from the fireplace.*

It is **MYCROFT**. *He looks at* **WATSON** *dismissing the gun in his hand and then at* **HOLMES**.)

MYCROFT. Good Lord Sherlock don't tell me why you are dressed in that absurd disguise. I assume it has something to do with that theatrical rag you sent me not an hour ago.

*(***HOLMES** *removes something from inside his nostrils and also two small balls from his cheeks. He wipes his face with a handkerchief taken from his coat pocket and sits down to light his pipe.* **MYCROFT** *looks about the room and then chooses a chair in which to sit.* **WATSON** *has now understood what has happened and says,)*

WATSON. Holmes, I could have killed you.

*(***HOLMES** *holds up a hand, opens it and slowly drops bullets into the palm of his other hand.)*

HOLMES. Ah, your bullets. *(to* **MYCROFT***)* You read it?

MYCROFT. With some interest.

*(***WATSON** *takes the bullets and reloads his gun.)*

HOLMES. The audition listing?

MYCROFT. As you knew I would.

WATSON. Holmes, what is going on? What is the point of this bizarre charade?

HOLMES. In a moment Watson. Mycroft, I trust our intrusion of last month did not get you into trouble at the Club?

MYCROFT. Shots fired? Police running in and out? Blood on the carpet. Why should that cause me trouble at the Club?

HOLMES. You know I'm most sincerely sorry.

MYCROFT. I'm now on a list of those at the Club who bear watching for improprieties and association with questionable characters of low breeding.

HOLMES. Perhaps I might speak to some of the more prominent members.

MYCROFT. Not if you wish me ever to speak to you again.

HOLMES. I'll stay away.

MYCROFT. A carriage waits on Baker Street below. It will remain there till I have need of it. You know, of course, why I am here.

HOLMES. Certainly. Watson, put away your gun and I will explain. Can Mrs. Hudson be roused to bring some tea and whatever confections she may have baked?

WATSON. Not at this hour.

HOLMES. Pity. What is special about tomorrow?

WATSON. Special?

MYCROFT. Malcolm March is to be hanged at dawn.

(**HOLMES** *removes a folded sheet of paper from his pocket and hands it to* **WATSON** *who unfolds it.*)

WATSON. It's a newspaper clipping.

HOLMES. Of that I am well aware. An advertisement from The Thespian Chronicle. Are you familiar with the publication, Watson?

WATSON. Can't say I am.

HOLMES. It's a weekly publication, four sheets devoted primarily to advertisements for theatrical professionals, musical acts, stage hands, the like. I might have missed it had it not been for our clever young Charlie Chaplin. He has a sharp eye. Read what he directed me to.

WATSON. *(reading)* Wanted. For one morning's work. Excellent pay. Discrete actor to impersonate a well known London consultant. Applicants should be slightly over six feet, quite lean, with sharp, piercing eyes and a thin, hawk-like nose. Chin should be prominent and with a squareness which marks the man of determination. Appear at 13 Bellowdnes Road at Midnight on the 15th .

(**WATSON** *finishes reading and looks up.*)

HOLMES. What do you make of it?

WATSON. Make of it?

MYCROFT. Watson, that description is taken directly from your very first published tale chronicling my brother's descent into criminal drama. Whoever wrote that hoped that those who responded would be auditioning to play Sherlock Holmes.

HOLMES. The fact that my name is not mentioned, that the pay is to be high and it is a singular performance suggests...

WATSON. ...a possible nefarious purpose, but it could also be some kind of prank or even a promotion for a public house or...

HOLMES. It could be many things, but combine the ad with the letter urging me to an intrigue in Glasgow, an intrigue that would have me on a train at the very moment my double was to be chosen, and we have a most promising situation.

WATSON. Promising what?

MYCROFT. Malcolm March has vowed that Sherlock will die before he dies.

WATSON. But he is safely in jail. What could he possibly do.

HOLMES. That is what I was determined to discover. I told you and Mrs. Hudson I was on my way to Glasgow. I even boarded the train and traveled one stop, on the chance I was being watched. I then hurried back to London by coach to audition for the role of...

WATSON. Sherlock Holmes.

HOLMES. The most difficult deception of my career, the ultimate challenge.

WATSON. I can't see why? You simply...

(**HOLMES** *begins to pace.*)

HOLMES. Nothing simple about it at all. I had to assume that whoever had placed that ad was quite familiar with my countenance, had seen me, watched me closely. Imagine for a moment that you were called upon to masquerade as John Watson, M.D. What would you alter? Are you aware of how you walk, how you cock your head to the right when you are puzzled, as you are doing now?

(**WATSON** *straightens his head.* **MYCROFT** *is sitting quietly apparently almost asleep.*)

HOLMES. *(continued)* Can you alter your speech slightly but not too much? And how do you alter it without losing the necessary resemblance to yourself?

WATSON. Most confusing. But why not simply go to the address and confront whoever was there. I would gladly have joined you.

MYCROFT. And you would have discovered nothing.

HOLMES. When we walked through the door, whoever was there would almost certainly have a covering story, a feeble one perhaps, but no law would have been broken. No, if I were to discover what this was about I would have to play the role. It was almost certain a crime was in the offing and I was to be a part of it.

WATSON. And so you donned the disguise.

HOLMES. And so I did.

(**HOLMES** *smokes and looks at the fire. The lights begin to dim till the stage is almost dark except for a few embers in the fireplace.*)

I arrived at Bellowdnes Road just before midnight ... There were two others seeking the role. The first was lean with a frequently broken nose bent over to the left deviating his septum and making his decidedly Cockney accent difficult to understand.

Scene Two

(This can be played to one side of the stage which is now dimly lit. **HOLMES***, back in his disguise, enters and joins two men lined up in front of a plain wooden table. Behind the table sit a* **MAN** *and a* **WOMAN***. The woman has a scarf draped over the lower half of her face. The men standing next to Holmes are tall and thin and there the resemblance to Holmes ends.)*

NICHOLAS. You, I want to hear an imperious 'You see but you do not observe.'

*(***FIRST APPLICANT***, in a decidedly cockney accent.)*

FIRST APPLICANT. You see but you don't observe.

ROSE. Can you do it without the accent?

FIRST APPLICANT. Accent?

NICHOLAS. Thanks.

(He tosses **FIRST APPLICANT** *a coin.)*

Sorry, you don't quite fit the bill. Show yourself out.

FIRST APPLICANT. I can do a bit of dancing and carry a tune.

*(***FIRST APPLICANT*** *does a bit of soft shoe, hands in pockets.)*

ROSE. Sorry.

*(***FIRST APPLICANT*** *shrugs, examines the coin, is satisfied, and departs.)*

ROSE. *(continued)* You. 'You see but you do not observe.'

SECOND APPLICANT. *(Posh accent)* 'You see but you do not observe.'

NICHOLAS. Less Duke of Pudding.

*(***SECOND APPLICANT*** *clears his throat and tries again. It is only slightly better.)*

SECOND APPLICANT. 'You see but you do not observe.'

*(***MAN BEHIND TABLE*** *reaches into his pocket for coin.)*

SECOND APPLICANT. I've done Shakespeare.

(**MAN BEHIND TABLE** *tosses coin.*)

NICHOLAS. I'm sure you have.

(**SECOND APPLICANT** *looks as if he has more to say but holds his tongue, clutches the coin and departs.*)

ROSE. That leaves you. You know the line.

HOLMES. You see but you do not observe.

NICHOLAS. Again.

HOLMES. You see but you do not observe.

(**WOMAN** *and* **MAN** *confer quietly.*)

ROSE. Experience?

HOLMES. As an actor?

NICHOLAS. What else?

(**HOLMES** *shrugs.*)

HOLMES. We did a couple of theatricals in Dartmoor. I played a doctor and an MP.

ROSE. What were you in for?

HOLMES. Why?

NICHOLAS. You want the job?

HOLMES. I was in for breaking into a jewelry shop.

NICHOLAS. Quick, how much is three hundred sixty three times seventy two?

(**HOLMES** *considers if he should answer*)

ROSE. What is the point of that question?

NICHOLAS. Verisimilitude.

ROSE. No one is going to ask him how much three hundred sixty four times seventy two is.

HOLMES. It was three hundred sixty three not...

ROSE. The pay is forty quid. Twenty now and twenty more paid right here as soon as you get back from making your delivery. You dress in clothes we give you and do what you're told. No questions. We'll give you a cover tale if you get stopped.

HOLMES. What'll I be doing? Or is that a question I

shouldn't ask?

NICHOLAS. You'll be playing Sherlock Holmes. You know who he is?

HOLMES. Everyone knows Sherlock Holmes.

ROSE. You are to go to Dartmoor Prison at seven tomorrow morning. You identify yourself as Holmes, deliver a small vial of liquid to a prisoner named Malcom March in solitary confinement, who is awaiting execution. You know who he is?

HOLMES. He murdered two men.

NICHOLAS. *(sharply)* Holmes is responsible for March's capture. No one will question his wanting to have one last gloat especially when March says that he is expecting the great detective.

HOLMES. Didn't March vow that Holmes would die before he did?

NICHOLAS. He did, but now all he wants to do is beat the hangman. The vial you'll be delivering will contain a fast-acting, tasteless and lethal poison. You can hand it furtively or…

ROSE. No more questions.

(**HOLMES** *nods. The* **WOMAN** *holds out her hand and opens it, palm up to reveal a vial of liquid.*)

ROSE. *(continued)* Think of it as a favor to a condemned man.

NICHOLAS. An act of mercy.

ROSE. Thwart the hangman.

(**HOLMES** *takes the vial and holds it up. Lights dim and fade into darkness.*)

Scene Three

(The embers of the fireplace in Holmes' and Watson's apartment rise. **MYCROFT** *sits with his hands folded in his lap.* **WATSON** *takes out his pocket watch.)*

WATSON. Then you would be due at Dartmoor in less than four hours to deliver that...

*(***HOLMES*** *produces a small vial which he holds up between forefinger and thumb so the firelight illuminates it.* **HOLMES** *eyes* **WATSON** *momentarily, then flips off the cork top of the container, puts the vial to his lips and downs the contents.* **WATSON** *bolts out his chair.)*

WATSON. What kind of insanity is this? Do you have an antidote? We must induce vomiting.

MYCROFT. Doctor, please subdue the histrionics. They are uncalled for in this, and in fact all, situations.

*(***HOLMES*** *smiles, replaces the cork and hands the vial to* **WATSON.***)*

HOLMES. Watson, kindly refill this vial with claret. We may have use of it.

*(***WATSON*** *takes the vial.)*

WATSON. I must say, Holmes. You are absolutely gluttonous with self approbation at my expense tonight. You've obviously removed the original contents and replaced them with some harmless concoctions to stage this tasteless music hall turn.

HOLMES. I assure you that the liquid I just downed was the same as that which was given to me but a few hours ago. I do confess, however, that I opened the vial to smell the contents and taste a speck on the tip of my finger. Rum with a touch of quinine. Would you like a bit of claret, Mycroft?

MYCROFT. Yes, thank you.

*(***HOLMES*** *pours it for him.)*

WATSON. You were hired to deliver a harmless drink to a condemned man?

MYCROFT. No Watson. He was hired by a clever murderer to deliver himself up to be his final victim.

HOLMES. March knew I would not simply appear in his cell if he called upon me to visit him, but he also counted on my being intrigued by an elaborate scheme and my ego to lure me to his cell where he could make good on his vow to personally kill me.

WATSON. How could you be certain that March…?

HOLMES. I tracked down Chaplin who said the ad calling for an actor who resembled me had been brought to his attention by a tall man with a Cockney accent and his nose broken to the left.

WATSON. Extraordinary coincidence. The very man you saw trying out for the role?

(**MYCROFT** *shakes his head in disbelief at Watson's failure to understand.*)

MYCROFT. There are no coincidences. The Calcutta episode was excused by the German Ambassador last night as a coincidence. Amusing and revealing.

HOLMES. May I explain, Mycroft?

MYCROFT. Certainly, but I suggest brevity over drama. The sun will not slow in appreciation of your performance.

(**HOLMES** *is amused.*)

HOLMES. Coincidence? Hardly. Charles Chaplin was chosen to bring that ad to me. And the ad was designed to intrigue me and lead me to the cell of Malcolm March who has had nothing to do but await execution and plan his revenge. Now I must go.

WATSON. To Dartmoor?

HOLMES. To Bellowdnes Road after I take care of the tall gentleman with the broken nose who is lurking in the street below to be sure that I appear at Dartmoor and that the show is on.

WATSON. I'll bring my revolver.

HOLMES. No my friend. You wait here for my return. I don't want to frighten the man with the broken nose into fleeing.

MYCROFT. Sherlock, be especially careful in the next several hours.

WATSON. I don't like your going about this alone.

HOLMES. It's the best way to trap the quarry below.

*(**HOLMES** puts on his cape and deerstalker hat, smiles at Watson and Mycroft and exits. **MYCROFT** puts on his glasses and reaches for one of Watson's medical journals.)*

WATSON. I don't like it.

MYCROFT. *(reading)* Do you doctors really think you can cure plague by inhaling aloe?

WATSON. How can you think of the plague when your brother may be in mortal danger?

MYCROFT. My dear doctor, it is precisely when we are in mortal danger that it is best to think of the plague.

*(**WATSON** paces. **MYCROFT** reads.*

***CHAPLIN** bursts in and looks around. He is somewhat agitated.)*

CHAPLIN. Where's Mr. Holmes.

*(**MYCROFT**, still reading, raises a hand.)*

No, Mr. Sherlock Holmes.

MYCROFT. Doing battle with a windmill I expect.

WATSON. He is out. What's the trouble?

CHAPLIN. The Irregulars have been watching this place, sort of keeping an eye on Mr. Holmes what with Crazy March going to die and all. And Docks Arnold sees Broken Nose Toole lurking across the way, figures we should put down on him so Docks runs for me and here I am.

WATSON. The effort is appreciated, but Mr. Holmes is fully aware of Mr. Toole's presence. He has gone out to apprehend him.

CHAPLIN. You're missing the bloody point.

(**MYCROFT** *looks up from the journal he has been reading.*)

Broken Nose Toole's game is lurking and luring. Gets his mark to follow him and then turns and does him in with a Holywater sprinkler. He means to do in Mr. Holmes. Let's go.

WATSON. A Holywater sprinkler?

CHAPLIN. A right cudgel with nails.

(**WATSON** *moves to the desk.*)

Hurry it on. You comin' Mr. Mycroft?

(**MYCROFT** *puts down the journal, removes his glasses and rises.*)

MYCROFT. My carriage awaits.

(*The stage goes dark.*)

Scene Four

(Blackness. The sound of a fog horn. A lamp now dimly illuminates the murky street. The set is minimal –the lamp, a storefront perhaps, a doorway. **BROKEN NOSE TOOLE** *enters from Stage Left and keeps walking till he exits Stage Right.* **HOLMES** *now enters from the left. Fog horns.* **TOOLE** *hurriedly appears from Stage Right, stops and confronts* **HOLMES** *who stops a few feet in front of him.)*

TOOLE. What game are we playing here?

HOLMES. Trap the criminal.

*(***TOOLE** *laughs, pulls a nail-spiked cudgel from behind his back and advances on* **HOLMES.***)*

TOOLE. I'm up for it. March is going to be disappointed he wanted to dance you down himself.

*(***TOOLE** *is no more than four paces from* **HOLMES** *when* **WATSON** *appears from Stage Right, gun in hand aimed at Toole's back.* **CHAPLIN** *appears next to* **WATSON** *with* **MYCROFT** *at his side.*

CHAPLIN. He swings from the left, Mr. Holmes.

*(***HOLMES** *bounds forward, ducks right under a swing from* **TOOLE,** *throws two punches to Toole's middle and then alternately punches with a right and left hand to the man's face. The cudgel falls to the street and* **TOOLE** *falls back in a sitting position, a look of astonishment on his face.)*

WATSON. Rather a dangerous move. I've witnessed your pugilistic skills before, of course, but it was lucky…

*(***HOLMES** *cuts* **WATSON** *off by handing him the cuffs.* **WATSON** *Cuffs* **TOOLE.***)*

HOLMES. Luck Watson? Since when have you known me to rely on luck? The man clearly favored the left hand as young Chaplin pointed out. I therefore moved to his left, delivered a blow to his kidney and another to his solar plexus, directly at the juncture at which….

MYCROFT. You may enjoy nights like this, but you know full well that I do not. The next time you feel you need help in apprehending a criminal, think of someone other than me.

CHAPLIN. Don't they both talk elegant Dr. Watson?

MYCROFT. I'm going to drop the young man on Baker Street and wend my way home on the nocturnal wheels of my awaiting carriage.

CHAPLIN. See what I mean?

(MYCROFT and CHAPLIN move stage left. CHAPLIN takes MYCROFT's hand. They exit. HOLMES, WATSON and TOOLE bent over in pain move toward stage right.

HOLMES. It was evident that his lungs would give up much of their supply of air. He was quite helpless when I delivered the next two blows to vulnerable nerve centers.

(Their voices fade a bit as HOLMES, WATSON and TOOLE move to exit.

WATSON. *(with a touch of sarcasm)* Forgive me Holmes. I should never have assumed you might need my help.

HOLMES. On the contrary, Watson, were I facing a firearm I would have welcomed your shooting him squarely between the shoulders. I'm an observer of human anatomy and a consulting detective, but I am no fool. We had best find a constable now to take our prisoner. Our game is far from ending.

Scene Five

(Still night. **HOLMES** *and* **WATSON** *stand outside a door on Belowdnes Road.)*

WATSON. Won't they have cleared out?

HOLMES. Why should they? I'm not due to make my appearance at Dartmoor till seven and should Malcolm March fail to kill me, Broken Nose Toole was to do the job. They are waiting for confirmation of my death. The end of the case is at hand, but there is one more bit of business as you know. Are you prepared?

WATSON. Yes, yes, of course but...

HOLMES. Check your watch Watson and join me in this performance.

*(***WATSON*** *checks his pocket watch.*

HOLMES *tries the door handle. It is locked.* **HOLMES** *knocks loudly. The door opens to reveal* **ROSE***.)*

ROSE. What are you doing here?

*(***HOLMES*** *holds out the vial.* **ROSE** *holds her voice in check as she says,)*

ROSE. We're not buyin' any potions today unless you guarantee it'll cure the pox.

WATSON. It will certainly put an end to far more than the pox.

ROSE. You're talkin' mumbo-jumbo.

HOLMES. So you deny knowing what is in this vial?

*(***ROSE*** *folds her arms.* **NICHOLAS** *is nervous.)*

ROSE. Em-phat-i-cally.

HOLMES. And you do not intend to either confess or tell us if Malcolm March has one more diabolical trick to play.

*(***ROSE*** *is determined, silent.)*

HOLMES. Watson, what time is it?

*(***WATSON*** *looks at his watch.)*

WATSON. Two minutes to seven.

> (**HOLMES** *appears to be nervous as he says,*)

HOLMES. If you tell us what he is planning, perhaps we can suggest that the law go easy with you. If not...

ROSE. I can't be bluffed Holmes.

NICHOLAS. For God's sake, Rosey, tell him.

ROSE. Pa-thet-ic bluff.

HOLMES. Quick Watson, the time, the time.

WATSON. One minute to seven.

HOLMES. Would you prefer the gallows.

NICHOLAS. They're not bluffing Rose.

ROSE. Let's hope they are Nicholas and be ready to have a drink with the devil if they're not.

WATSON. Whatever March is paying you woman, is it worth dying for?

HOLMES. March is paying them nothing. This lady is Malcolm March's sister or first cousin.

WATSON. How do you know?

> (**HOLMES** *moves quickly, grasps her left wrist and holds up her hand.*)

HOLMES. The Milverton fingers.

WATSON. Good Lord!

HOLMES. Some imprints cannot be discarded. Time Watson?

WATSON. *(looks at his pocket watch)* Seven.

ROSE. He's beaten you Holmes. Malcolm has a small bottle of real poison hidden in his cell. My brother is probably dead as we speak. He may not have bested you, but he has beaten the hangman.

HOLMES. Not completely. Watson, the real time?

WATSON. Six o'clock.

ROSE. You're still too late. You will never get to Dartmoor in time.

HOLMES. Quick Watson, we haven't a moment to lose.

(WATSON *and* HOLMES *exit. A* POLICEMEN *enters.*
ROSE *finally crumbles.* NICHOLAS *puts a comforting
hand on her shoulder. Stage right we suddenly see the
silhouette of* MALCOM *and the bars of a prison window.*
MARCH *removes a small bottle from the darkness and
holds it up. The light from first rays of morning illumi-
nate it and it alone.*)

Scene Six

(HOLMES and WATSON enter hurriedly and look at the barred window of March's cell.)

HOLMES. Time Watson?

(WATSON shows HOLMES his watch and exits. HOLMES crosses to the prison cell door, careful not to get too close.)

MARCH. Do you have the time?

HOLMES. Nearly seven.

MARCH. No. I mean 'Can you spare the time?' You are the incredibly busy Sherlock Holmes.

HOLMES. I can spare the time.

MARCH. You did not attend the trial other than to give preening testimony. You were not present for my remarks though the court cut me short before I could say very much.

HOLMES. You now wish to present your defense?

MARCH. No Holmes. I am defenseless. I wish to address your guilt. But first a question.

HOLMES. Yes?

MARCH. What are you doing here?

HOLMES. Seeing that you do not thwart justice.

MARCH. You are not here in the name of justice. You are here to relish the final moments of your adventure.

(HOLMES has nothing to say.)

You murdered my father.

HOLMES. Your father was…

MARCH. …the worst man in London. I know. That is what you said Dr. Watson dutifully recorded your comment as if it were of a Biblical judgment. My father was a petty blackmailer, no more, but you stood by and watched that wretched woman kill him. Tell me. Did you consider it an execution and yourself the judge?

HOLMES. You murdered innocent people March.

MARCH. Yes, but how many deaths of innocent people like my father are you responsible for. Who are you to accuse me of insensitivity? You prefer bees to people.

HOLMES. With a few notable exceptions.

MARCH. My father took care of my sister and me. He took money from guilty people who could afford it. He murdered no one. You needed a monster and my father was at hand.

(A clock begins to strikes.)

HOLMES. Is there anything you would like me to do?

MARCH. Yes, die before I do.

HOLMES. I shall be unable to accommodate that request. But...

(HOLMES *holds up the vial of claret.* **MARCH** *holds up his vial of poison.)*

MARCH. 'He does not feel that sickening thirst That sands ones throat, before the hangman with his gardener's gloves comes through the padded door. And binds one with three leathern thongs.'

HOLMES & MARCH. "That the throat may thirst no more."

(They toast, and both drink from their vials.)

HOLMES. You have been a worthy competitor. I live only to play the game.

MARCH. And I shall die only because I played it with you.

(MARCH *backs away from the cell door. The clock strikes the seventh and last time.* **HOLMES** *is alone on stage.)*

HOLMES. "He is at peace -the wretched man At peace or will be soon: There is no thing to make him mad, Nor does Terror walk at noon, For the lampless Earth in which he lies Has Neither Sun nor Moon."

Scene Seven

(**HOLMES** *and* **WATSON**'s *rooms. The place is dark except for the light of the fire in the fireplace. In fact, the stage looks exactly as it did to start the play.* **HOLMES**' *voice is raised.* **HOLMES** *paces.*)

HOLMES. And so, Watson, March's flare for the dramatic and his obsession with poetic revenge proved his undoing though he did defeat the hangman, you see.

(**WATSON** *enters through the open door of his room. He is obviously tired and perhaps a bit irritable.*)

WATSON. No, I do not see, Holmes and at the moment I do not wish to see. I wish to change my clothes and go to bed.

(**WATSON** *removes his shoes.* **HOLMES** *paces, full of energy.*)

HOLMES. Watson, the further one is removed from an event the less he will remember of it, a precise account of this tale is of the essence. I will help you.

(**WATSON** *has his shoes in his hands.*)

WATSON. I'm going to sleep Holmes. Historical accuracy may suffer a bit, but it will be far less than if I were to listen to your observations now. The sun is up. Good morning.

(**WATSON** *goes to his room and closes the door.* **HOLMES** *shakes his head, moves to the window, pulls open the thick curtains to let in the morning light and looks out toward the street below.*)

HOLMES. Why aren't you home in bed?

(**CHAPLIN** *appears from the armchair, the back of which is facing us and Holmes. It is precisely the same move Holmes made at the beginning of the play.*)

CHAPLIN. How'd you know I was there?

(**HOLMES** *folds his arms and looks at* **CHAPLIN**.)

HOLMES. The dirt on the street where we captured Broken Nose Toole was laced with brick and mortar from a house being built at the corner. The dirt clung to your shoes. I saw traces as we entered. Mycroft's footprints came in and went out. Your footprints stayed in.

CHAPLIN. If you'd learn me, I mean teach me, how to do that, I could make a rum living off it somehow.

HOLMES. Stick to the stage like your mother and father though it may not hold the promise of wealth, you seem to have a talent for the theatrical.

CHAPLIN. Make you a deal, you teach me some of that observing stuff and I'll teach you how to dance.

HOLMES. No.

CHAPLIN. Give it a go. What's it hurt?

HOLMES. Why aren't you at home?

CHAPLIN. What's it hurt?

HOLMES. Your mother had a hard night?

CHAPLIN. They're all hard. She seeing things again. Me and Dad'll probably have to get her back to hospital today.

(*Pause.*)

HOLMES. All right. We'll try it.

(**CHAPLIN** *moves to the center of the room and does a few little steps.*)

CHAPLIN. Give it a go.

(**HOLMES** *tries it. He's not bad. Music Hall music, the same song we heard Entre'act earlier, perhaps 'Any Old Iron' again rises from nowhere. Side by side* **CHAPLIN** *and* **HOLMES** *execute the same step.* **HOLMES** *smiles.*)

Again.

(*They repeat the step several times.* **WATSON** *appears in the doorway of his room trying the sash of his robe.*)

WATSON. Good Lord. Can we not put an end to this adventure?

HOLMES. My dear Watson, this is the end.

(**HOLMES** *and* **CHAPLIN** *keep dancing.* **CHAPLIN** *slowly spins around. So does* **HOLMES**. *The spin ends with* **CHAPLIN** *and* **HOLMES** *facing the audience.*)

Curtain

PROPS

221B Baker Street
Watson's Desk and Chair
2 High-Backed Arm Chairs
Umbrellas and canes in an umbrella stand
Cabinet/side table with a chair
Watson's Journal
Ink pen and well
Small tray of 7 pastries
Pipe
Persian slipper with pipe tobacco
Paper
Violin and Bow
Plate of 6 sandwiches
Napkin
Cane
Loose sheets of paper
Mantle Clock
Decanter of Claret on a sliver tray
2 Claret glasses
Medical Magazine
Humidor
Unanswered Correspondence
Jackknife (holding corrspondence to fireplace)
Revolver for Watson
Bullets for revolver
Newspaper clipping

Thrace's Room
Bed
Bedside table
Rug
Tea cup and saucer
Gun
Death threat
Knife rigged to stick out of actors neck

Diogenes Club
2 Easy Chairs
Side table
Rug

Chinese puzzle box
Book with ribbon marker
Decanter of sherry
2 glasses
2 firing Derringers
March's Gun
Bellowdnes Road
Plain wooden table
2 plain wooden chairs
2 coins
Actor's resume
Vial of poison

The Street
Fence with bushes
Nail spiked cudgel
Hand-cuffs

Prison
Cot
Vial of poison

COSTUMES

SHERLOCK HOLMES
Dress shirt
Red smoking jacket
Grey jacket
Vest
Black pants
Black dress shoes
Disguise -
Brown coat
Brown vest
Brown pants
Tie
Inverness Overcoat
Brown socks & shoes w/
  lifts
Make-up–Nose spreaders
Deerstalker hat

WATSON
Dress shirt
Brown jacket
Brown vest
Brown pants
Gold cravat
Brown socks
Dark shoes
Smoking jacket

MARCH
Dress shirt
Brown jacket
Vest
Brown pants
Tie
Brown socks & shoes
Hat
Suspenders
Disguise –
Dress shirt
Grey vest
Black cutaway coat
Cravat
Grey pants
Black shoes
Grey wig
Grey beard
Glasses

THRACE
Blue pj's
Blue velvet robe
Blood red cravat
Black socks & slippers

REGINA
Corset & Petticoat
Black maids dress
White apron
Knee highs
Black boots
Mop cap
Black purse

TIM ELLY
Brown pants
Brown shirt
Vest
Tie
Socks
Brown boots
Cap

JACK DAWES
Henley
Grey pants
Vest
Brown jacket
Socks
Brown boots
Cap

CHARLIE CHAPLIN
Dress shirt
Black tail coat
Black knickers
Neck tie
Black knee socks
Black boots
Black bowler hat

MYCROFT
Dress shirt
Vest
Grey cutaway coat
Grey pants
Tie
Black Socks & shoes
Pocket watch

ROSE
Corset &Petticoat
Red bodice
Red skirt
Black boots
Wig
Lace fan
Black purse

NICHOLAS DRAGLETON
Dress shirt
Jacket
Vest
Pants
Tie
Black socks & shoes

TOOLE
Grey Henley
Brown shirt
Grey jacket
Brown pants
Tie
Brown boots
Hat

ACTOR/SECOND APPLICANT
Dress shirt
Jacket
Vest
Pants
Tie
Black socks & shoes

BOBBY
Uniform Jacket
Pants
Belt
Black socks & shoes
Hat
Night Stick

STUART KAMINSKY is author of 50 published novels, 5 biographies, 4 textbooks and 35 short stories. He also has screenwriting credits on four produced films including *Once Upon a Time In America, Enemy Territory, A Woman In The Wind* and *Hidden Fears.* He is a past president of the Mystery Writers of America and has been nominated for six prestigious Edgar Allen Poe Awards including one for his short story "Snow" in 1999. He won an Edgar for his novel *A Cold Red Sunrise,* which was also awarded the Prix De Roman D'Aventure of France. He has been nominated for both a Shamus Award and a McCavity Readers Choice Award. Kaminsky writes several popular series including those featuring Lew Fonesca, Abraham Lieberman, Inspector Porfiry Petrovich Rostnikov, and Toby Peters. He has also written two original Rockford Files novels. He is the 50th annual recipient of the Grandmaster 2006 for Lifetime Achievement from the Mystery Writers of America.

Other plays by **STUART KAMINSKY**

Books

Please visit our website **samuelfrench.com** for complete descriptions and licensing information

www.ingramcontent.com/pod-product-compliance
Lightning Source LLC
Chambersburg PA
CBHW070406120726
47909CB00005B/1658